Every Song a Vengeance: Poems

Table of Contents

Act One

Think of John Wick, in the Club,
about to Take More Revenge than Most Ever Get

Grief sneaks up on you
not the big rolls of shock,
the tidal waves of how will I live
but rather those small, odd bit
flotsam and jetsam of a life you lived
before
> John Wick moves through crowds, parting them
> with a knife, a gun, a well placed fist,
> you imagine that he must once have moved
> fast, tenderly too
> The puzzle of a fight scene is trying to remember
> that every fighter once loved someone or
> loves someone
still
there are times when a thing as simple
as tea with too much honey, a joke told
in a certain way, can make you stumble
out of the now, how easy it is to forget
you are forgetting until you
don't
> forgive, is the motto of the movies, don't try
> to move past what breaks us, fight it
> John Wick doesn't blink, grief made machine,
> rising from the ground, hands opening in the dark
> like praying in rewind

John Wick Watches Another Zombie Movie

And they're just people
shambling ahead, arms outstretched
as if they want to grab on to someone
else's hand, to hold on for dear afterlife

The dead want to tell us things:
secrets like how we can't just
keep going forward, like how
there can be pleasure in stopping

Zombies don't remember the people
they once were, though they might
still look like the one you love

There are so many almosts
like the way a face in
dreams almost looks like someone
you've lost, like the way we almost
are good
at going on, at surviving this

Maybe if we asked them, the dead
would speak. Maybe they'd tell us
all the things we should focus on
instead. Maybe we never learn
to take as much
as the dead
are willing to give.

John Wick and Baba Yaga Walk Into a Bar

What myths we make of men
who fight. How we prize their hands,
their fast feet.
In stories of Baba Yaga, she's a witch,
the big bad at the end of it all. But
there is kindness there to, in how she keeps
the tongues of liars, how she cradles the memories
of the dead every night, rocks them to sleep.
A man who can make himself disappear is just
doing what every woman has already
learned. How to vanish is not
as hard as how to unvanish, to step
into the light, to make yourself
stand out, a house on chicken legs,
a fence made of skulls. Sometimes we need
to yell in order for people to hear
us whisper.

John Wick, in the Classroom, explains his Pedagogy

If you were meant to be taught
you'd want to be taught
by the sound of someone

telling you they want you to keep
going. You'd want someone
who understands that movement

and silence are not mutually
exclusive, that sometimes you
can get back up after you fall

off buildings, through glass,
through ceilings. You'd want
someone who understands

pain, knows the shape of how
something hurts, the way grief
can be a weapon or

even, sometimes, a way to not
be a weapon. If you want to be
taught, you want to learn, and

learning is best done by
whatever means necessary.

Even sometimes

by hoping you never
have to learn.

John Wick Ends Up in a Taco Bell Wondering Where To Go Next

We've all been there,
 at midnight, waiting between
sleep and running, between having been
somewhere and going somewhere
else. Time doesn't exist

in towns with fast food restaurants,
lit up in the dark
how the signs all look
like they belong to another
era, not the past,
but not the future either,
just something other

Inside, no one is sleeping
but no one wants to be awake.
The menu shines
names of things you've heard
of but don't believe exist—
each a misremembered take
on food belonging to
someone else.

When the food comes,
it tastes hot and salty
and every crunch
between teeth
is a reminder that you
are still here
wherever here
is tonight.

Guns. Lots of Guns.

John Wick says
But what he means is: god,
I'm so tired

At some point, who hasn't
Asked for what we no
Longer want

Desire and desperation
Are like sisters who love
One another but no longer
Can stand the sound of the other's voice

At some point, we all ask
For more

As if by asking, by knowing
We think
We might finally
End

Act Two

In Which We Let John Wick have a Little Coffee, as a Treat

John Wick orders a grande, because he mixes up
which one is large and which one is medium,
again. He gets it with sweet cream, so he
can watch the pattern it makes as it blends.
　　　He doesn't think of how the reactions of the cream and the coffee are
like two bodies caught in battle, how they both tangle and disorder each other
until they are one single thing.

John Wick doesn't get a pastry, but he'd like one,
would like a croissant that is still warm from the oven,
the cracking crumb as he breaks it open with his hands,
the warm smell of yeast, butter, flour baked.
　　　Sometimes he thinks about how his hands break open other people's
worlds, how his hands have also pet dogs, soft dogs with droopy ears and big
dogs with low growls, and how his hands have also held guns, and also held his
wife's hand. How his hands contain multitudes.

John Wick takes a moment to still his body,
sitting in the light, at a table warmed
by the sun, by his cup of coffee, by his
hands pressed against the top, he takes
a sip.
　　　Once, years before, his wife had sat across from him, in a café, at a
table, staring out the window, just over his shoulder, watching something
outside and away from him. He'd taken a sip of his coffee, and that had been
his life. Then. For a moment. How they could both be together in their separate
thoughts. How their separate thoughts could both be about something so simple
as the way the sun came through the window just right. It bounced off the
surface of their coffees, reflected the light up and up.

John Wick can never sit for long,
leaves before anyone's noticed
he was there. Just an empty
cup, a chair pulled slightly
out of place. Like everyone moves
eventually.

John Wick Does a Crossword Puzzle, While Waiting for Revenge

1 across: the name of your childhood best friend

There's a moment, always, between doing and seeing
the body understands before we do
to catch that falling glass, to
step out of the way of that bike coming our way.
to understand that we've lost something

2 down: the number of people you have to get through to find some semblance
of peace.

How many of us know how many times we've lost
ourselves? In childhood, when we learn
truths behind magic: the trick
is to watch the hands. As adults,
the trick is to watch
the eyes.

3 down: why 2 down is a trick question

When do we stop what we know
we didn't want to start
How much of our lives
is learning to live
with ourselves

5 down: how long you will grieve

There's no outside
to what we remember.
Just there, just all around,
just always.

John Wick Plays a Song by Sufjan Stevens on the Jukebox

It is all tunnels
of memory

How grief still sounds
like grief even
when it's a melody

Sadness when sung
still feels as if you
can stab yourself
with it

If you could give a name
to everything you lose
would it make a good
album title?

Maybe a life unlived
sounds like half of half
a measure

But maybe that's too
pretty to be true

A song can sound
like memory

like grieving
if you forget
the words

John Wick Never Books First Class

There's a simplicity to this
How we place our safety
In arithmetic:
Only a small amount of planes
Crash, only a small amount
Of people might take
Another life, only a
Small amount of mistakes
Are fatal, only
That doesn't mean anything

When it's you on the plane,
At the other end of someone's
Anger, taking the wrong turn
On a road slicked with ice

We call ourselves lucky
When we have near misses,
When we find ourselves on the right
Side of Chance's equation

But that's not such simplicity
The arithmetic of life
And its multiplications
Of mood and weather
And engine malfunctions
And precision and every
Small thing that has to go right

In order for us to make it
Home each day. The
Division of our lives is

How

How lucky we are
That we can place
Our safety
In anything

Portrait of John Wick as an Object

Keys will leave you wanting
something of their own.
There are no locks they will
not covet, feverishly metal
hot, and turning

into something else. Freed
they will discover that form
is water, shape is ghosts
who can't remember their own
names, and you

are stone struck buildings
with windows but
no doors. Keys will leave
you wanting. Keys will
leave you locked.

John Wick Finds Shapes in Clouds

A cloud, on average, might weigh one
million pounds
How something so seemingly made of nothing
can add up
This tastes like I'm eating a cloud
a friend once said about a seven minute
icing—that fluff and push of egg whites, sugar,
time

As a child, I used to measure the sky
cloud by cloud
pinching my fingertips around
the shape, trying to space out what
they each might be
Now I point out one that could be
a dragon. You still do that? someone
says

Clouds are just air and water
our bodies are mostly water too
maybe that's why we think
of heaven as clouds, of ghosts
as vapor-like, intangible, hard to
reach out and touch

On a plane once, the clouds
outside looked thick as snow, some
winter landscape
as a child I used to build tunnels
from the snow, placed myself
inside, the cold could seem
so warm

What could we measure against
a cloud? The shape of our bodies
falling in love, the movement of
our hands when we reach out,
how something so seemingly
nothing still adds up

Bogeyman

There's two possible ways to trace the word
one is that it is something scary,
a word to frighten awake your children
The other is that it is a word like
a scarecrow, it keeps the bad away.
A child wandering too close to the water
is told about La Llorona, ready
to grab them into the river, pull them down
to her embrace. We don't say how she was
once a mother, how she's just waiting for
her child's warmth.
A child prone to mischief
is warned about the things
in the darkness, how they slip out
at night. We don't say how lonely
the shadows can be, how deep
the corners of empty rooms.
We never think about
how no one tells stories
to the bogeyman,
 so they don't get lost
in all that dark, themselves.

John Wick finds a twenty-dollar bill on a sidewalk

All luck finds its balance
in the caught glass rolling
from a table edge or
the bus missed by a minute

Not the diagnosis
the leaving
some things we can't assign
to four-leaf clovers
and losing streaks

When a black cat crosses
your path, you should always
look the other way

like at train crossings
or holding your child's hand
on streets
when they are small enough
to still hold on

your mantra becomes
look

both ways
as if danger
is always visible

The things we see coming
if we just turn
fast enough

John Wick Gets Lost in a Corn Maze Outside Reedsburg, Wisconsin

Viewed from the sky, all plots of land look
As if they could belong to anyone
All cornfields carved with purpose
Seem like they were painted
By time and heat
And the rain

A man could get lost out here
But it's not meant as threat
But rather some kind
Of benediction

How you enter the maze and
Can cheat, can slip through
Stalks if you want to take
The straightest path
But what's the fun

In finding your way
If it means you stopped
Understanding the shape
Of unfinding, of twists
And turns, and retracing

The steps you took to
The ones you meant
To take

A truth about corn
Is the cobs bind your
Insides and the silk
Unlooses them

Two ills that Each
Cure the other
As if all loss
Has something to find
As if all mazes
Are their own answer

Act Three:

I'm Thinking I'm Back

in style, in business, in your mind

I'm back as a philosophy:
one where you do what you
have to and pretend it's what
you need.

I'm back as in a
comeback, a retort,
a thing you meant to say
but didn't but should
not have anyway.

I'm back to face
the music, to bring everything
to light. I'm back as

a cliché. As it is what
it is because at the end
of the day, I'm what
you want.

I'm back from the dead
from the store
from work
from war
from everywhere
you thought I was lost.

I'm back to tell you
just one thing:

that there is so much
in this world that we
can't take hold of, so much
that we need to fight against,
that you will feel like
you might never sleep, you might
just want to scream and
scream into the dark.

But, I'm back,
I'm here
and you're here

and that's
almost
everything.

John Wick as Ghost Story

Some nights you wake up,
positive that the one you love
is sitting in the dark beside
you as a ghost. You never
turn to look though and so
they've never died.

He asked,
once, if you believed always
that the ghosts of the living
would come for you. You tried,
hard, not to nod.

She asked,
maybe twice, if you were afraid
of the living dead, those
zombies coming back. You
shook your head.

You almost always want
to turn, to see the one you love,
though in dreams she never
lives. You wake up often
to the ghost beside you
weeping. One of you
is weeping.

You answered,
just the one time,
that you'd never fear
something you'd been for
so long.

John Wick, On a Beach, After the Fall of Civilization

Water forgives without
calculations.
The lost and losing
baptized into waves.

In folktales, women can shed
their animal skins, be brought
in from the sea. Their bodies
forget but their tongues still

crave salt. In no myths,
are men once animals
who can be tamed.

They stay as wolves,
jaguars, beasts,
who know to hide
their teeth.

Water breaks the body
down slow.
Bones kept pristine,
memories of lives
once battled.

Those carried on waves
know how the world moves
without ceasing.
How teeth come
in all sizes.

How sharp
the shallows can be.

John Wick Dreams of Dogs

Large-eyed dogs in fairy tales
        are sometimes helpful
                but more often wicked
They follow, chase, frighten
        Padfoot and Gwyllgi
                and Gytrash
                        and others
Whose names have been
        forgotten, misused, rewritten
                too many times in too many ways
They steal, slobber, trick
        saucer eyes and thick black fur
                footprints in the mud as big
                        as a bear's, a wolf's, a lion's
The splish-splosh behind each
        wary weary wayward traveler
                is like an execution signed off
                        the governor turns off the phone
                                the switch about to be thrown
Still when I saw you there
        dinner-plate eyes downcast, tired out
                cleaning your paws in the corner
I reached out
        to feel your tongue against my hand
                warm warm warm

If I were a monster

I'd be the type to live

in lakes, come up from
the dark when I want
to see the stars

I'd imagine every way
I'd lose you
because monsters must
tell stories too

to their children, to
the ones they love, they must
whisper about all the things
that could go wrong

Isn't that how we know
we're human? That we
tell stories to keep
away the night?

There are so many monsters
we count up
As children, they were easy

to spot. Now, they are
the man behind us, the
mold inching through
our walls, the things

we fill our oceans with

A group of monsters
should be called

a possibility

John Wick Meets Ted "Theodore" Logan

There are two sides to every coin
even the ones you cash in
for what you're owed

If one side is vengeance
than the other side must be
to forgive, to be

excellent to one another.
If your heart breaks
then there must have been
a heart to begin with.

Imagine a future in which
everyone can travel to their
pasts. How much would
we try to warn ourselves
or stop ourselves or would

it all just be us: looking at
our pasts with such tender
love that we can hardly
stand it? We were there

were there

we are here.

Portrait of John Wick as an Astronaut

Deep in darkness
                        outer space falling through
you can close your eyes
and lose all sense
of where your body is positioned
in space
                        and here, here, that has multiple meanings
a lack of proprioception
the coordination of movement
the knowledge of your own body's
motions can be catastrophic
                        on Earth, you can become trapped in your own body
there is such effort
in reaching out, in taking
a step, standing still even,
that we don't think about,
don't have to think about
                        in space, spinning, you can close your eyes
sometimes, as a child,
you'd think about breathing
and find it hard to do and, in terror,
once you woke from a dream where
your body forgot how to take air in,
exhale
                        you can close your eyes and forget
a lack of proprioception can pull
you out of your mind, even if only
for a moment, and you think
how hard it is to reach out
                        in the dark, in the open, in the expanse
the world moves and we don't
know, can't feel it, and we

move, we feel each movement
                    and in the dark, you can't grasp what it means

John Wick Plays as John Wick in Fortnite

Haven't we all wanted to climb outside
ourselves and see
what everyone else is seeing?

You can be on a team,
can listen to everyone
even after they're dead.

How they tell you to
look out, do a dance,
grab that shield.

They call your character
your skin. How odd
to be under it and still
see yourself. Know the movements
of your body
on the screen.

When the game glitches,
when you walk into walls
over and over
or see through walls
as if staring at the
future and
it's still just fighting
and running
and trying to get past
the oncoming storm.

At the beginning of the game,
you have to jump from a balloon,

have to watch your body
twisting down towards
war. Once you've jumped
you can't stop. There is no

undoing even here.

John Wick Writes a Single Love Poem

When I am a ghost, I will
remember the time you held
my hand as we swam in the coldest
part of the coldest lake
we had ever known

I will haunt only
the cities I have never lived
in, afraid of frightening
anyone I might once
have loved

As a ghost, I will
be saddest about never
having to eat
even the memory of how
you fed me chocolate will stale

When I am a ghost, I will
count, on my non-existent
fingers, all the times
I forgot to say
something sweet to you

A Poem in Which John Wick Dies

Except he doesn't
John Wick lives out his days
In retirement, somewhere warm
With the sound of waves and
A lizard that skitters across the tops of his bare feet
When he sits on his porch

John Wick's feet are callused
And scarred but
The lizard doesn't notice
And John wick no longer
Notices either

Sometimes his ankle aches
When it rains, sometimes his
Shoulder is stiff and he can't reach
The things on his highest shelves

Not the books, not the photos
He means to dust, not the multitude
Of mundane
Things he keeps

Like we all keep
Our homes filled
With the memories
We think we want
And the useless things
We forgot we kept

Even John Wick, one day,

Is old enough to hold
His life around him
As if it is no longer

Fragile enough to break,
When he's not looking,
As if that is all
We've ever wanted

John Wick Tells You a Ghost Story

I think you can tell a lot about a person by
the faces they expect to see out darkened
windows, under the bed, in the very back
of the closet. The ghosts we keep close

tucked into our pockets, the way we sign
our names, the color we think of when told
to imagine something peaceful; these are the ones
we need to exorcise every day. The ghosts that come

back to us sometimes in dreams, usually we see
them across crowded streets and yell out their names
but the trouble with common names
is that you can't turn every time you think someone

might be calling for you. There's always someone
calling out to you. And in dreams these ghosts
never remember us, they shake their heads when
we open our arms to embrace them.

And, somehow,
that's enough.

"Think of John Wick, in the Club, about to Take More Revenge than Most Ever Get" in *Drunk Monkeys*
"John Wick and Baba Yaga Walk Into a Bar" in *trampset*
"John Wick, in the Classroom, Explains His Pedagogy" in *Porcupine Literary*
"John Wick Gets Lost in a Corn Maze Outside Reedsburg, Wisconsin" in *Maudlin House*

A huge amount of gratitude to Freddy and Vegetarian Alcoholic Press. A more supportive publisher is hard to imagine. Thank you for asking to look at a collection of weird John Wick poems and seeing something there.

To the editors, staff, and readers, at the magazines where some of these pieces originally appeared, many thanks for all you do to support the literary community.

Thank you to Keanu Reeves and the John Wick creators for creating art that sparked the imagination. I'm sorry or you're welcome for the way in which I interpreted your creation.

Giant thanks to those who have been there alongside me, your support means the world: Gillian Ramos, Matt Paul, Hannah Grieco, KC Mead-Brewer, Maria Rago, Lisa Koca, Crystal Stone, Chris Corlew, Jeni De La O, Zara Chowdhary, Philippe Meister, Kanika Lawton, Jennifer Fliss, Rita Mookerjee, Gretchen Rockwell, Jonathan and Jayvian Antunes, The Martins Families, Nicole Oquendo, Maggie Cooper, M. Molly Backes, and everyone who has been kind.

To those who I would put in my own Continental of awesome, so much love: Stephanie Gunn, Bronte Wieland, Erin Schmiel, Hannah Cohen, E. Kristen Anderson, Teo Mungaray. And to my family with more love than even John Wick has vengeance: Brian Ramos, my parents, brothers, nephews, and Gramma Millie.